The
Poky Little Puppy's
First Christmas

by **Justine Korman**

illustrated by **Jean Chandler**

A GOLDEN BOOK • NEW YORK
Golden Books Publishing Company, Inc., New York, New York 10106

When the winter sun peeked through the window of the McCraes' house that morning, four little puppies tumbled out of bed and played until it was time for breakfast.

Polly, Penny, Pickles, and Pat ate at four bowls in a row, their four little tails a-wagging.

"But where in the world is that poky little puppy?" their mother wondered.

Poky was still fast asleep. His mother nudged him and said, "Come on, Poky. Today is Christmas Eve!"

Poky yawned and stretched. Even on a special day like Christmas Eve, he was still poky.

Four little puppies rode on a sled pulled by Tommy McCrae. But where in the world was the poky little puppy? He was saying good-bye to his mother. Poky promised he wouldn't be late. Then he ran across the yard to follow the sled.

At the edge of the yard was a gate, and outside the gate was a meadow. Across the meadow was a forest—crowded with Christmas trees!

The McCraes were going to the woods to find a tree.
Poky wasn't sure why the family wanted a tree, but so far
he loved Christmas Eve! The snow was white and bright,
and it tickled his nose.

Once he was in the woods, Poky sniffed a strange smell.
He forgot about keeping up with his brothers and sisters.
He even forgot to watch where he was going.

Poor Poky tumble-stumbled, slipped, and slid down a deep, dark hole! "Help! Help!" he cried. Wouldn't someone come to help him out of the slippery, slidy hole?

"I'll help you," said a friendly voice. "My name is Herman."
Poky looked up to see a young skunk peering over the
edge of the hole. Then Herman climbed down into the
hole beside Poky. Soon he was pushing Poky from behind
and helping him to climb up. Before long the two of them
were out of the hole.

"You smell funny," said Poky.

Herman sniffed. "You smell funny, too," he said. "Let's have some fun!"

He led Poky up a winding path and down a hill to a frozen pond. Then he showed Poky how to slide back and forth across the cold, shiny ice.

What fun! Poky remembered his mother telling him that Christmas Day was even better than Christmas Eve. But Poky couldn't believe anything could be better than this!

Not far away through the wintry woods, the McCraes were having fun, too. Tommy pointed to a fir tree beside a hollow log. "There's the perfect tree!" he exclaimed. His sister, Kate, agreed.

Mr. McCrae raised his axe and whack, whack, whacked until—CRACK—the tree fell. It fell over onto the old hollow log, and the four little puppies barked excitedly.

Poky heard Pickles call, "Poky! Come on, Poky!" He remembered his promise not to be late. But he wondered if he would see his new friend again.

"It's easy to find me," Herman said. "I live in a hollow log just over that hill."

Poky ran up a hill and down another and through the snowy woods toward home. Suddenly he saw something in the snow and stopped. Poky sniffed the strange object up and down and all around.

He had found an old red rubber boot. The boot was too wonderful to leave behind, so Poky dragged it out of the woods, across the meadow, and into the McCraes' yard.

"I told you not to be late!" Poky's mother scolded gently when he came through the gate.

"Look what I found!" Poky exclaimed.

His mother shook her head and said firmly, "You can't take that messy, muddy old boot into the house."

Sadly, Poky left the boot by the garden gate.

After a tasty supper the puppies helped decorate the
Christmas tree. Poky sniffed at the fragrant green branches.
Penny nibbled a strand of popcorn.

When the tree was glowing with winking, blinking
lights and shimmery, shiny glass balls, Poky's mother told
her puppies all about Christmas. "And to celebrate this
special day, we give each other presents," she said at last.

"Will we get presents, too?" asked Penny.

"Look under the tree tomorrow morning, and you'll find
out," said their mother. Then she sent the puppies to bed.

Poky, of course, was the last to reach the cozy cushion where the puppies slept.

His brothers and sisters soon fell asleep, dreaming of rubber balls, biscuits, and bones. Poky stayed awake thinking sadly about his red rubber boot.

On Christmas morning the puppies raced to the tree—and found the presents that they wanted.

"A toy mouse!" Penny cried.

"A fluffy stuffed bear!" Pat exclaimed.

"Mmm, a biscuit," said Pickles with a sigh.

Polly chased a brand-new bouncing ball.

Poky tore open his big package. "My boot!" he cried happily. "And it's all shiny and clean!"

After breakfast a gentle snow started to fall. Poky's brothers and sisters went off to play in the meadow.

"Please don't be late for Christmas dinner," said Poky's mother.

Then Poky ran out the gate, across the meadow, and into the woods to find Herman. The skunk was nowhere in sight, so Poky followed his nose.

It took a long time, but Poky finally found a wet, cold, and miserable Herman.

"What happened?" Poky asked.

Herman said sadly, "I'll show you."

Poky followed the skunk up the hill to the hollow log that had been Herman's home. The McCraes had crushed it accidentally when they cut down their Christmas tree.

Poky felt sorry for Herman. The little skunk was alone in the cold, snowy woods, and he had no home. So Poky took Herman home with him through the woods, across the meadow, and through the garden gate.

Poky's mother was amazed to find that her puppy had made friends with a smelly skunk.

But Poky's mother felt sorry for Herman, too. That night she let him sleep in the doghouse she and her puppies shared in the summer.

And Poky gave up his warm, cozy bed in the McCraes' home to keep his friend company in the doghouse.

The next morning the most amazing thing happened.
The poky little puppy was the first one out of bed.

"Where in the world is that poky little puppy?"
everyone wondered.

The puppies and their mother and Herman followed
Poky's tracks in the cold, crunchy snow. They went out the
gate, across the meadow, and right to the edge of the
wintry woods.

Poky saw his family and called, "Come and look! Look
at Herman's new home!"

"Why, it's your boot!" Poky's mother exclaimed.

"Go on in and try it," Poky told Herman. And the skunk wriggled into the cozy, dry boot. "Merry Christmas, Herman!" said Poky. "Even if it is a day late."

Poky's mother was very proud of her puppy. It was only his first Christmas, but Poky had already learned that the best gifts of all are the ones you give.